Dedicated to Mom, Sharon, Paul, Christine and Alison.

Thank you for always believing in me and pushing me to go for my dreams. If you dare to imagine, you will discover endless opportunities.

PDhyms.

Lumpy the elephant loves to play.
He climbs a tree most every day.

How can he do that, how can it be?
Well Lumpy is extraordinary!

He wasn't always like that you see,
Sit back and I'll tell you the whole story.

It happened once upon a day
Sometime in April or in May

Lumpy was overheard to say
" Why must I be an elephant today?

Frumpy and dumpy and grumpy, am I"
He said with a moan, a groan and a sigh

" Elephants are just no fun,
All we do is walk and run.

We cannot fly or even swing,
In fact, we can't do anything.

Wouldn't it be nice to be a monkey?
I could climb and swing on any tree."

So he tried all day to climb those trees,
He bruised his nose, he bumped his knees.

His tail was too short, his nose too long.
His plan had a flaw, something was wrong.

"If I can't be a monkey, I'll be a giraffe,
If I wish real hard perhaps, perhaps."

And so he wished with all his might
To grow his legs and neck that night

But his mother whispered in his ear
"Be careful what you wish for dear.

It's not what's on the outside you see.
It's what's on the inside that matters to me."

She gave him a kiss and sent him to bed,
But Lumpy didn't listen to what she said.

So when he went to sleep that night,
The fairies came to him in flight.

"We've heard your wishes and seen your dreams.
You don't want to be an elephant it seems.

We are here to grant your wish.
Do you want to be a fish?

Or would you rather be a bear.
They sleep all winter without a care,

ZZzZZz

Or bird or lion, whatever you wish,
Have you considered a rhinoceros?"

RRooAR

And so he thought for quite a while,
Until he finally cracked a smile.

"At last I know what I shall be!"
He said to the fairies gleefully.

They tapped their wands, then went away
And soon the night turned into day.

Sad Lumpy was nowhere in sight.
What had happened to him that night?

No one could find him, where did he go?
What did he wish for, they needed to know.

Then all of a sudden, what did they see?
An elephant sitting upon a tree.

"Oh Lumpy what have you become",
Said his friends, his dad, his mom.

Lumpy jumped down from the tree,
Light as a feather he seemed to be.

"I am still an elephant, yes it's true!
But now I am neither sad nor blue.

I decided that if I just tried to be me,
I could do things that were extraordinary.

So I could have been a bear, a fish,
A monkey, even a rhinoceros.

But Lumpy the elephant I will stay
And be the best I can each day.

So when I awoke, I climbed that tree.
I just went about it differently.

I used my nose, my legs and tail,
Believing that I would not fail.

So I have a message for all of you,
When you are sad and feeling blue.

Be careful when you make a wish,
You might wake up to be a fish!

And if those fairies should come to you,
In a dream when you're sad and blue.

What you should say is, 'I like being me'
Because that is what makes

YOU

extraordinary."

The End of the Story

(But the beginning of Lumpy's new adventures!)

Start your own adventure.

Write or draw pictures of your dreams. Remember that you are EXTRAORDINARY TOO!!!!!!

Dream #1

Dream #2

Dream #3

Dream #4

Dream #5

Dream #6

57354696R00015

Made in the USA
Charleston, SC
11 June 2016